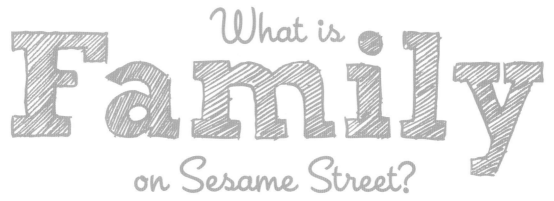

What is Family

on Sesame Street?

Words by Craig Manning
Pictures by Ernie Kwiat

When you think of a "family," what comes to mind?

How would you describe it? Which words do you find?

No exact meaning quite fits like a glove.

Except maybe this one: it's all about LOVE.

From the day you are born, your family is there,

to protect and support you, and show you they care.

They raise you and teach you, and watch as you grow,

and do what they can to let their love show.

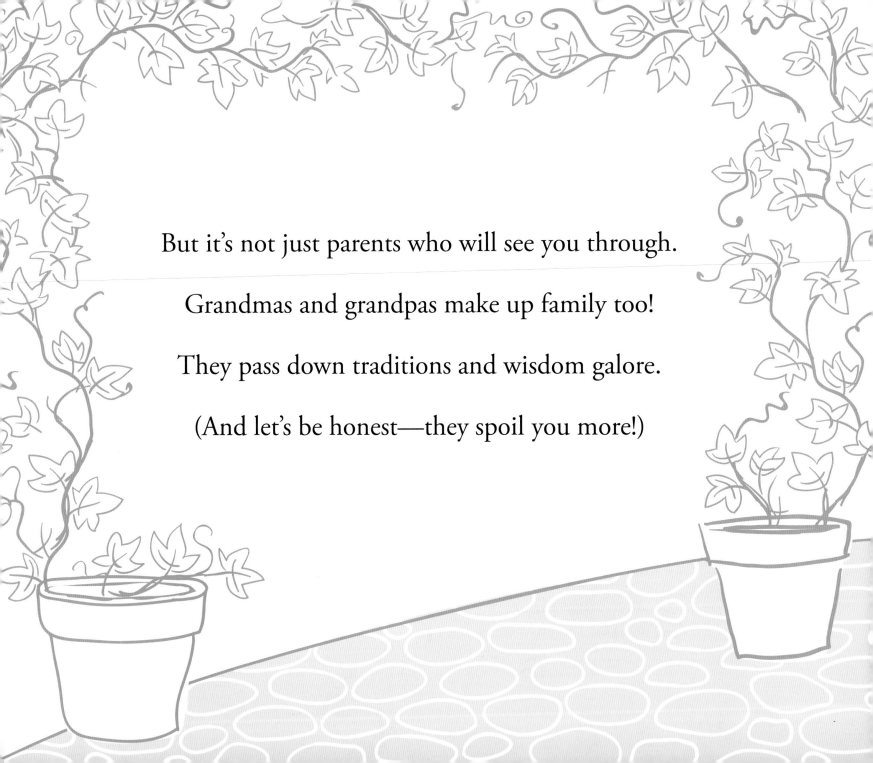

But it's not just parents who will see you through.

Grandmas and grandpas make up family too!

They pass down traditions and wisdom galore.

(And let's be honest—they spoil you more!)

Some families are large, while others are small,

but it's not about size or numbers at all.

A family can add up to any amount.

What matters is making "together time" count!

Sometimes a family's a party of two:

that one special person you love most…and you!

Someone you can run to, who makes it okay

if you stumble a bit or have a bad day.

A good time with family can take any form.

You can play together quietly, or dance and perform!

You can fill your days with fun and the silliest songs.

When it comes to family, there's no right or wrong.

All families are colorful in their own way,

from pink, green, and blue, to white, black, and gray.

Each canvas is different, a true work of art,

with each face and voice playing its unique part.

What's better than sharing a smile with your mother?

Or giggling along with your dad and your brother?

Families make memories by laughing out loud,

for laughter is best when it's shared with a crowd.

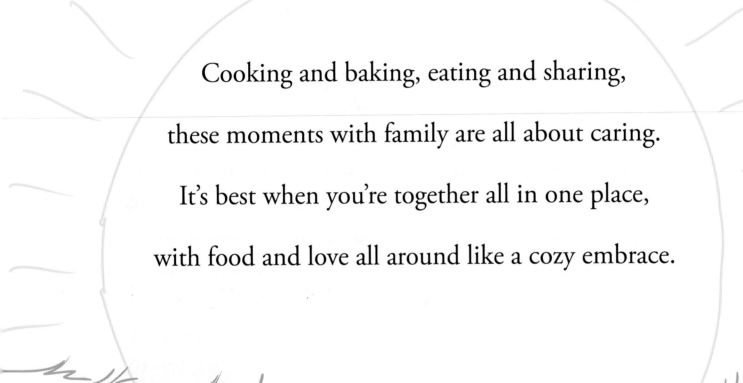

Cooking and baking, eating and sharing,

these moments with family are all about caring.

It's best when you're together all in one place,

with food and love all around like a cozy embrace.

There will be days that you spend far apart,

but *familia* is always right there in your heart.

And letters and phone calls or chats on a screen

can shrink all the miles stretched out in between.

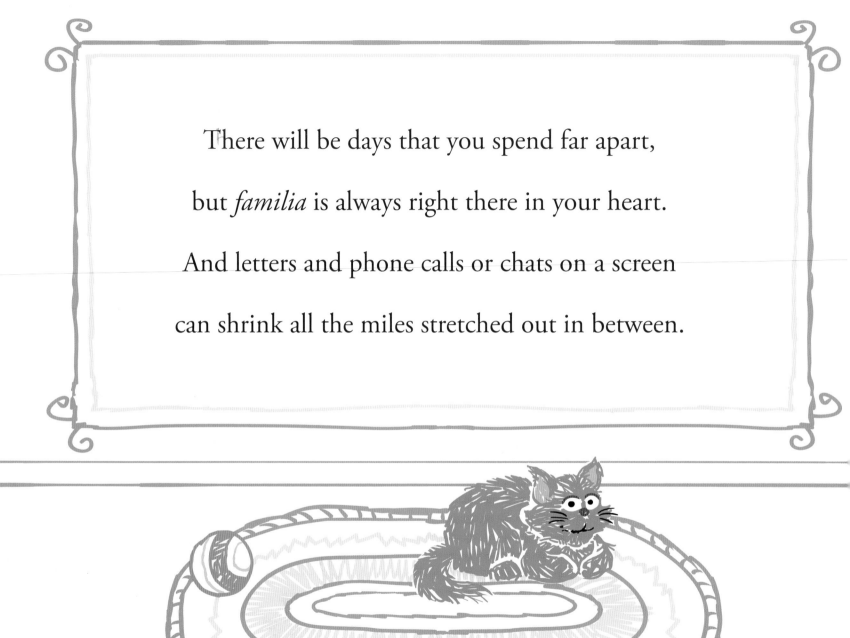

Families can change and evolve now and then.

New members may join, and you'll gain a new friend!

Having new siblings or more than one home

just means love goes with you, wherever you roam!

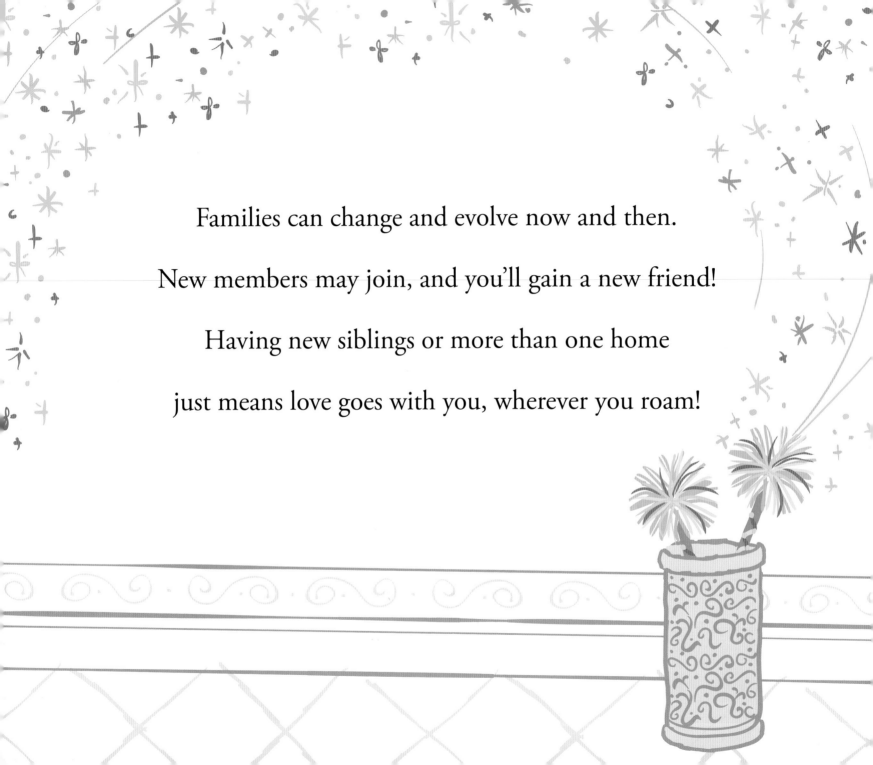

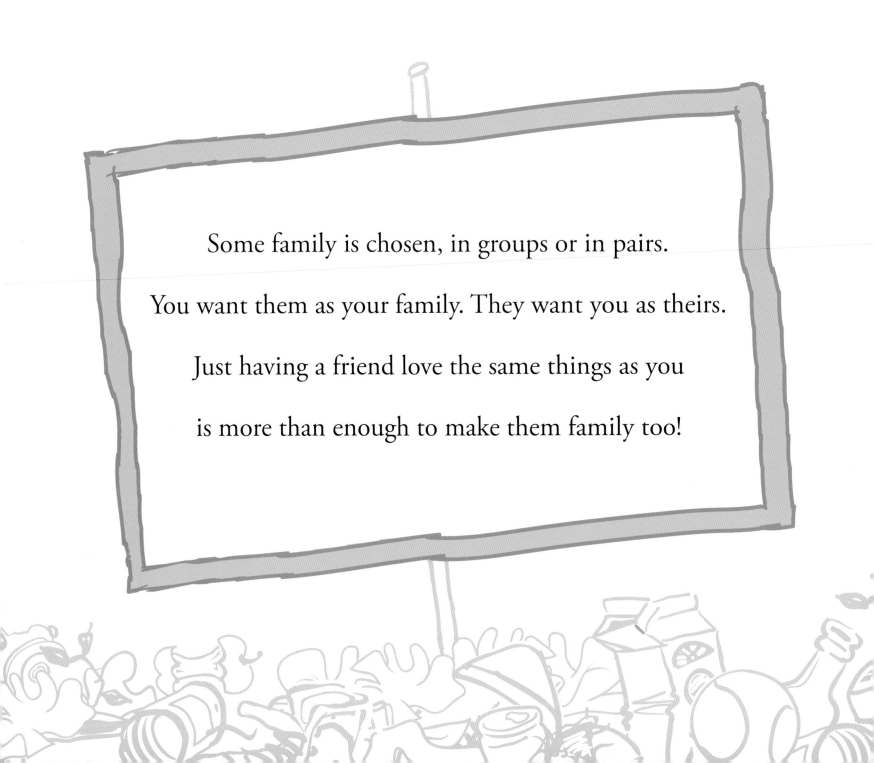

Some family is chosen, in groups or in pairs.

You want them as your family. They want you as theirs.

Just having a friend love the same things as you

is more than enough to make them family too!

The older you get, the more you will see

so many new branches on your family tree.

Like an oak or a willow, love grows as it should,

till your family includes your whole neighborhood.

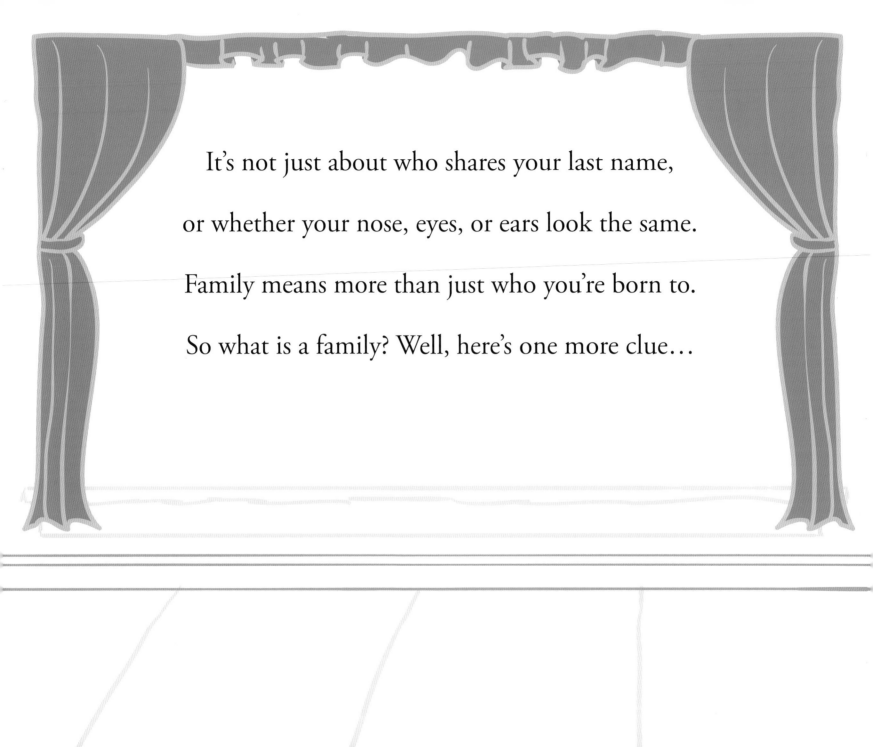

It's not just about who shares your last name,

or whether your nose, eyes, or ears look the same.

Family means more than just who you're born to.

So what is a family? Well, here's one more clue…

It's your **parents** and grandparents, **siblings** and friends,

and the love that you feel as every day ends.

It's a hug or a high five, or a song that you sing.

A HOME is love, hope, and family, and that's everything.

Cover and internal design © 2020 by Sourcebooks
Text by Craig Manning
Illustrations by Ernie Kwiat

Sourcebooks and the colophon are registered trademarks of Sourcebooks.

Published by Sourcebooks Wonderland, an imprint of Sourcebooks Kids
P.O. Box 4410, Naperville, Illinois 60567-4410
(630) 961-3900
sourcebookskids.com

Source of Production: 1010 Printing Asia Limited, North Point, Hong Kong, China
Date of Production: December 2019
Run Number: 5016829

Printed and bound in China
OGP 10 9 8 7 6 5 4 3 2 1